Bedtime stories for children

Collection of short bedtime stories for children

By

Susan Walker

Table of contents

Introduction

A fantastic one-on-one activity that fosters your child's creativity, language abilities, and listening is reading bedtime stories. By establishing this habit, you may boost your child's brain growth while also teaching them how to follow directions and unwind before bed.

Children's bedtime stories can range from those that are entertaining, colorful, and exciting to those that teach kids how to handle issues or overcome obstacles but still have a happy conclusion. Your youngster will learn about life through bedtime stories in a kind, delicate, and engaging way.

Chapter 1

The Unwise Emperor

An emperor who didn't care about ruling his realm once lived. Instead, his only concerns were living in his palace, indulging in the best food and beverages, gathering the most expensive possessions, and, above all else, dressing as gorgeous as possible.

One day, some thieves arrived on the land. They claimed to have the finest cloth in the world, but it was magical, so they informed the emperor. Nobody who wasn't bright, intelligent, or influential could see it, only the smartest, most brilliant, and most influential people could.

The emperor was terrified when he was shown the fabric since he was unable to see anything at all.

He reasoned that if people learned that he wasn't brilliant, smart, or significant, they would choose a different ruler.The greatest things won't surround him, and he won't be the most significant person in the country.

The emperor then requested that they create an outfit for his great parade after informing the thieves that it was indeed the best fabric he had ever seen.

Everyone in the kingdom came to see the emperor on the day of the parade. They were all interested in seeing the miraculous fabric because they had all heard about it.

The great parade started, as the emperor made his way along the large National Mall. No one could see the supernatural attire, but no one dared to speak.

Then a young boy asked, "Why isn't the emperor wearing any clothes?" while pointing at the monarch.

This inspired others to be daring to speak up, and before long, the emperor's foolishness had virtually the entire kingdom talking. He chose to go down the street naked rather than telling the truth because he was too worried about valuable items, fashionable clothing, and people's opinions.

Chapter 2

The wish of the Stonemason

A stonemason who was not contented with his life once existed.

He said, "I wish I were the king," and then all of a sudden he was.

The stonemason soon realized that the king was always being interrogated and that he was required to work even when he wished to relax.

The stonemason remarked, "I wish I were the sun." "The sun is strong and doesn't listen to orders."

He became the sun all of a sudden. However, the stonemason quickly realized that clouds may weaken the sun's power.

The stonemason remarked, "I wish I were a rain cloud." They have sufficient strength to block out the sun.

Suddenly, he changed into a cloud of rain. The stonemason attempted to alter the shapes of the rocks as he showered down on the soil.

The stonemason said, "I wish I were strong enough to change the shape of rocks," and all of a sudden he was back to being a mason, ready to cut the stone and carrying a chisel.

He said, "I'm pleased to be a stonemason again." "All I need is the ability to turn stone into lovely things."

The lesson in this tale is to be careful with your wishes and to be grateful for what you already have.

Chapter 3

Changing Positions

There once was a family. The mother stayed at home and worked to take care of the kids and the house while the father went out each day to work on the farm.

The farmer once complained when he returned home that the house was not in order, the baby was wailing, there was no butter or bread, and his meal hadn't been prepared.

He scowled at his wife and questioned, "What do you do all day?" "I could work more efficiently than you do all week in one day."

Okay then, you take care of the house while I work on the farm," his wife replied.

That's was exactly what they did.

The man started his day by feeding the chickens and putting milk in the churn to make butter while the woman left early to work in the field.

But as the baby began to cry, he went to pick him up. Their toddler went into the kitchen, knocked over the churn, and milk spilled all over the place while the dad was calming the baby.

When the dad realized he hadn't served the kids their breakfast before starting to clean up the mess, he stopped. He started to prepare breakfast, but the chickens had entered the house and were scattering dung and feathers all over the place because he had neglected to close the door after feeding them.

It continued like this all day. Every time the farmer attempted to take action, he discovered other errors occurred.

The house was covered with feathers and chicken dungs when the woman came home from the fields. The kids had run through the milk, leaving a sticky, unpleasant trail. They were also hungry and filthy. She discovered her spouse holding a sobbing child while seated on the bed.

He apologized, "I cannot imagine all of the things you have to manage while working hard at home every day," adding, "I am sorry, darling wife. I promise never to complain again".

In addition, he would prepare dinner for the family, help with the kids, and churn the butter for the following day on the days he returned home with no food.

This story has just as much application today as it did then. Everyone's task could appear simple until you have to complete it on your own.

Chapter 4

Honesty is a virtue

A ceremony was held to select the next king because an old king had no child.

Every child who wanted to attempt would receive a seed, he ruled. The seed needed to be nurtured for a year at home. The best plant grower would be the new leader at the end of the year.

Matilda participated in the competition and took home a seed. She planted the seed in the ideal soil, gave it just the correct amount of sunlight, and carefully watered it.

Other kids in the community had little sprouts at the end of the first month, but Matilda did not. All of the other kids grew small, bushy plants by the third month, but even so, Matilda had nothing.
Because Matilda couldn't even grow a little plant, the other kids teased her and said she could never be the leader.

Matilda switched the container and dirt. At the end of the year, despite doing all she could think of, she still had nothing.

All the kids, with the exception of Matilda, brought their plants to the palace on the last day of the competition. She sobbed while sitting at home, but her parents urged her to be proud of her labor of love and accompanied her to the judgment.

The king inspected the lovely, lush plants as he strolled up and down; some of them even had fruit. He then made it to Matilda's.

Where is your plant, the king asked

Matilda cried while saying, "I worked extremely hard. I provided the seed with my best soil, irrigated it daily, gave it the ideal amount of sun, and brought it inside during the cold weather. However, nothing I tried could get the seed to sprout.

The king said, "That's correct, I distributed dried, boiled seeds to everyone. None of them were able to develop into plants"

The king added, "You are the only sincere child who had the courage to acknowledge that your seed wouldn't develop. You are now our new leader as a result of your honesty"

Chapter 5

The Mermaid's Ring

Unintentionally, a teenage fisherman once caught a mermaid in his net. According to legend, if you catch a mermaid and let her free, she will grant you one desire.

He wished that the girl he liked would always adore him.

Why do you like her, the mermaid asked. He replied to the mermaid and said "because she is the world's most beautiful girl."

After some consideration, the mermaid gave the boy a magical ring.

She instructed him, "Give this ring to the girl you want to spend the rest of your life with, but you have to wait a full year from today before it will work."

On his way home after accepting the ring, the kid met a homeless girl. She asked, "Please, sir, could you spare something to eat? I'll work for you in exchange.

Even though he didn't have much, the kid decided to give the girl some of his food in exchange for her aid in storing his nets. After sharing his meal, they parted ways, and the boy got into bed to dream about his love.

He shared his food with the girl and she helped him with the nets every day for a month. Then one day she suddenly disappeared. She was sleeping in his fishing hut when the worried lad went looking for her.

The boy felt guilty for never considering the girl's sleeping arrangements. He awoke her, allowed her to rest by his fire, and later built a room in his house for her. He assured her, "You can sleep here for the next 11 months." You'll have to go when my wife moves in, though, he said.

He was upset when the girl didn't show up the next day to assist him with his nets.

He said, "I provided her food and a room, and this is how she pays me back?"

He threw down the nets and stormed inside angrily. What the boy saw was so unbelievable. Never before had his tiny house been so tidy. A pot of stew was waiting for him on the fire, his bed had been made and cleaned, and there was a pile of chopped wood by the fire.

The boy felt guilty once more. The young woman put in a lot of effort all day to make his home a wonderful home.

Following their meal together, the girl went to her room, while the boy climbed into his freshly made bed and daydreamed of his love.

The lad would ask the girl to stay and talk as the months went by, and then they would both retire to their rooms for the night. The lad spoke of his love every night as they exchanged family-related tales.

Then, one morning, when the child woke up, he discovered the girl standing by the door, with her belongings.

Why are you doing that? asked the boy.

She said, "I must go, it is time for you to wed your love."

The boy was unaware that a full year had passed. In an effort to find his love, he snatched the ring and raced to the village. The boy realized she was exactly the same when he found her, but his feelings had changed.

He then took off for his house and pursued the girl.

She questioned, "Did you find your love?"

Yes and no, the boy replied. "In the village, I found a regular girl, but now that I am with you, I know I have found my love."

The boy gave the girl his ring, and they went on to live happily ever after.

Benefits of bedtime stories

Reading bedtime stories to your child may be the ideal way to spend some of your valuable time and attention with them, but did you realize that this straightforward reading practice has advantages beyond just helping them fall asleep? Reading bedtime stories to your child is a wonderful way to improve their learning abilities, from their brain development to language skills and vocabulary. Regularly delight your child with a wonderful bedtime tale, and you'll quickly observe these advantages.

www.ingramcontent.com/pod-product-compliance
Lightning Source LLC
Chambersburg PA
CBHW071507150726
48000CB00006B/2733